Together...

An Activity for School or Home

 Read the story aloud.

 Make a two-column list that tells what the vet checked on Ginger and what she found out. You can use the headings, "Checked" and "Found Out."

Level J
Factual Recount
Social Studies/Science

Ginn Reading Steps

Ginn

www.pearsoned.ca

ISBN 0-13-035829-0

9 780130 358295

Ginger's Checkup

Written by Kim Newlove • Illustrated by Bruce Armstrong

It was spring, and time for Dad and I to take our dog, Ginger, to the vet for her yearly checkup. Ginger doesn't like going, but I tell her it's for her own good.

3

We had to be at the vet at nine o'clock.
Dr. Yoon is Ginger's vet. She patted Ginger
gently on the head and talked to her.
Dr. Yoon knew she was nervous.

4

Ginger was shaking, so I stayed close to her and told her not to be afraid. I gave her a big hug.

Dr. Yoon looked at Ginger's teeth. "They look very healthy," she said. "Do you clean them?"

"Yes," I said. "Ginger doesn't like it, but Dad helps me. We also give her rawhide chew toys to help keep her teeth clean."

7

Dr. Yoon touched Ginger's nose. She told me it felt healthy and that a dog's nose should always feel damp and cool.

"It is," I answered. "Dad and I both check her nose often because you told us it is important."

Dr. Yoon used her stethoscope to listen to Ginger's heartbeat. She said, "It sounds healthy. She must be getting plenty of exercise."

"Dad and I take her for walks twice
a day," I told the vet. "And we make
sure she doesn't eat too much 'people' food!"

Dr. Yoon examined Ginger's feet. "They look
healthy too. There are no signs of any sores on them."

"We don't let Ginger walk where there might be broken glass," I said. "We clip her nails when they get long. Dad and I do this together. I hold Ginger's foot while Dad clips."

Dr. Yoon finished her checkup and told me that Ginger was in perfect health. "Keep taking good care of her," she said.

"Give her healthy food and fresh water. Take her for walks every day, even when it is raining or snowing."

Dr. Yoon told Ginger her checkup was all over.
She patted her and asked, "Would you like a biscuit,
Ginger?" Ginger wagged her tail. She wasn't
shaking any more!